STRANGER THINGS™

ZOMBIE BOYS #3

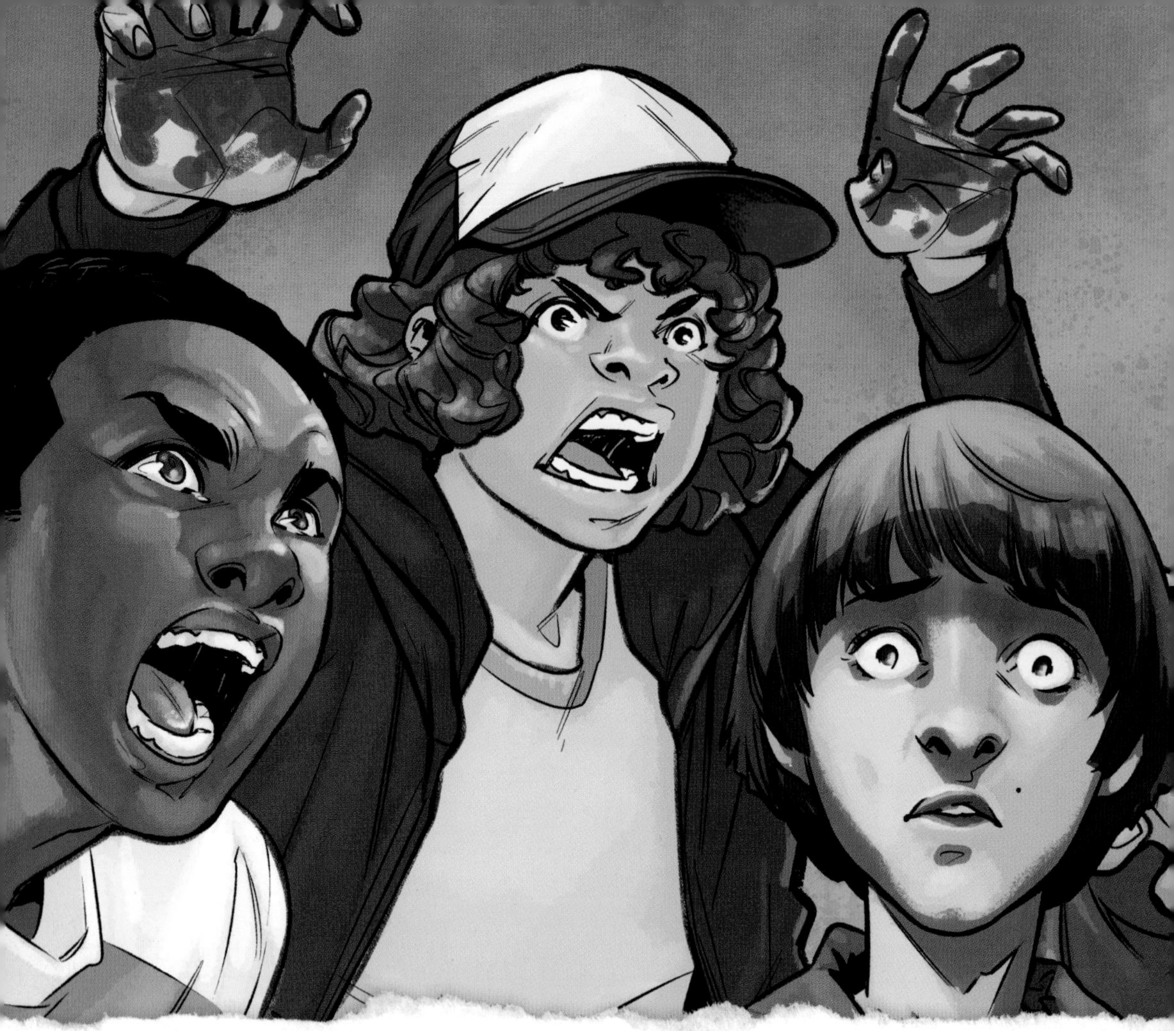

STRANGER THINGS™

ZOMBIE BOYS #3

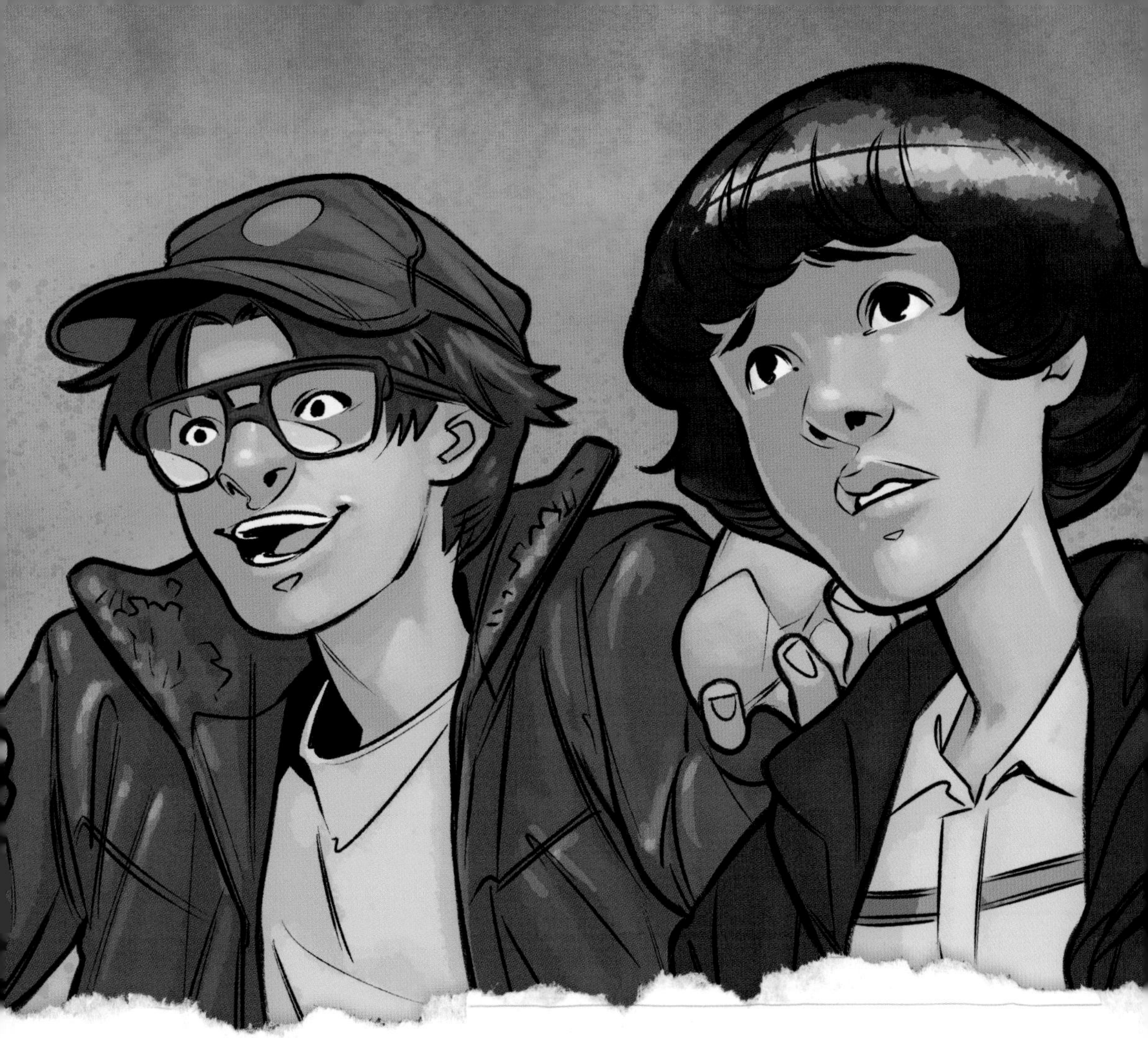

script by
GREG PAK

Art by
VALERIA FAVOCCIA

colors by
DAN JACKSON

Lettering by
NATE PIEKOS OF BLAMBOT®

cover Art by
RON CHAN

ABDO
Spotlight
DARK HORSE BOOKS

ABDOBOOKS.COM

Reinforced library bound edition published in 2022 by Spotlight, a division of ABDO,
PO Box 398166, Minneapolis, Minnesota 55439. Spotlight produces high-quality
reinforced library bound editions for schools and libraries.
Published by agreement with Dark Horse Comics.

Printed in the United States of America, North Mankato, Minnesota.
092021
012022

THIS BOOK CONTAINS
RECYCLED MATERIALS

DARK
HORSE
BOOKS

NETFLIX
OFFICIAL MERCHANDISE
©NETFLIX

Library of Congress Control Number: 2021939399

Publisher's Cataloging-in-Publication Data

Names: Pak, Greg, author. | Favoccia, Valeria; Jackson, Dan; Piekos, Nate, illustrators.
Title: Zombie Boys / writers: Greg Pak; art: Valeria Favoccia; Dan Jackson; and Nate
    Piekos.
Description: Minneapolis, Minnesota: Spotlight, 2022 | Series: Stranger Things
Summary: When a new kid to the AV club wants to make a zombie movie based on
    Will's drawings, the boys come to terms with the real horrors they've already
    faced.
Identifiers: ISBN 9781098250782 (#1, lib. bdg.) | ISBN 9781098250799 (#2, lib. bdg.) |
    ISBN 9781098250805 (#3, lib. bdg.)
Subjects: LCSH: Stranger things (Television program)--Juvenile fiction. | Science fiction
    television programs--Juvenile fiction. | Supernatural disappearances--Juvenile
    fiction. | Monsters--Juvenile fiction. | Zombies--Juvenile fiction. | Graphic novels--
    Juvenile fiction
Classification: DDC 741.5--dc23

Spotlight

A Division of ABDO
abdobooks.com

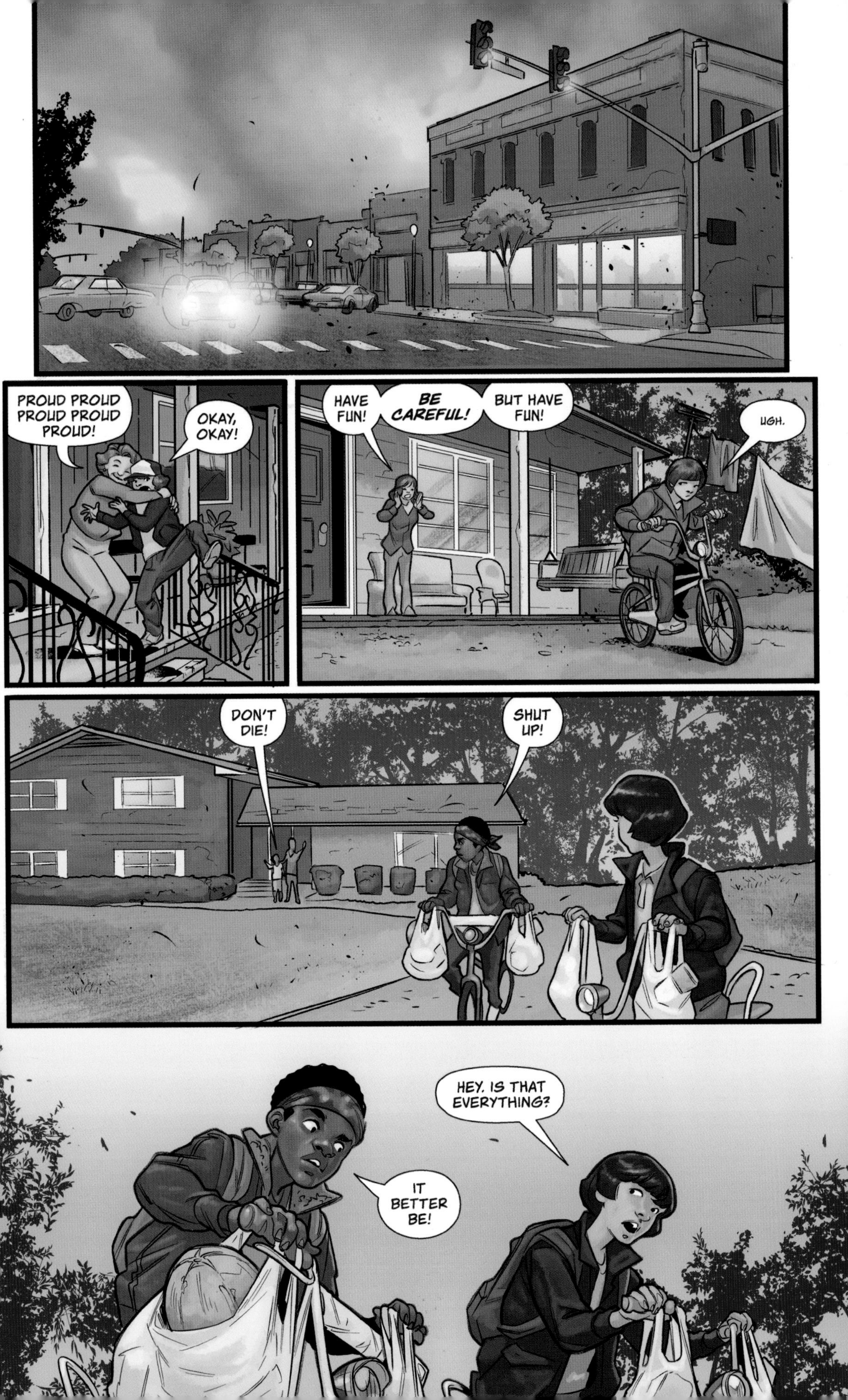
PROUD PROUD PROUD PROUD PROUD!
OKAY, OKAY!
HAVE FUN!
BE CAREFUL!
BUT HAVE FUN!
UGH.
DON'T DIE!
SHUT UP!
HEY. IS THAT EVERYTHING?
IT BETTER BE!

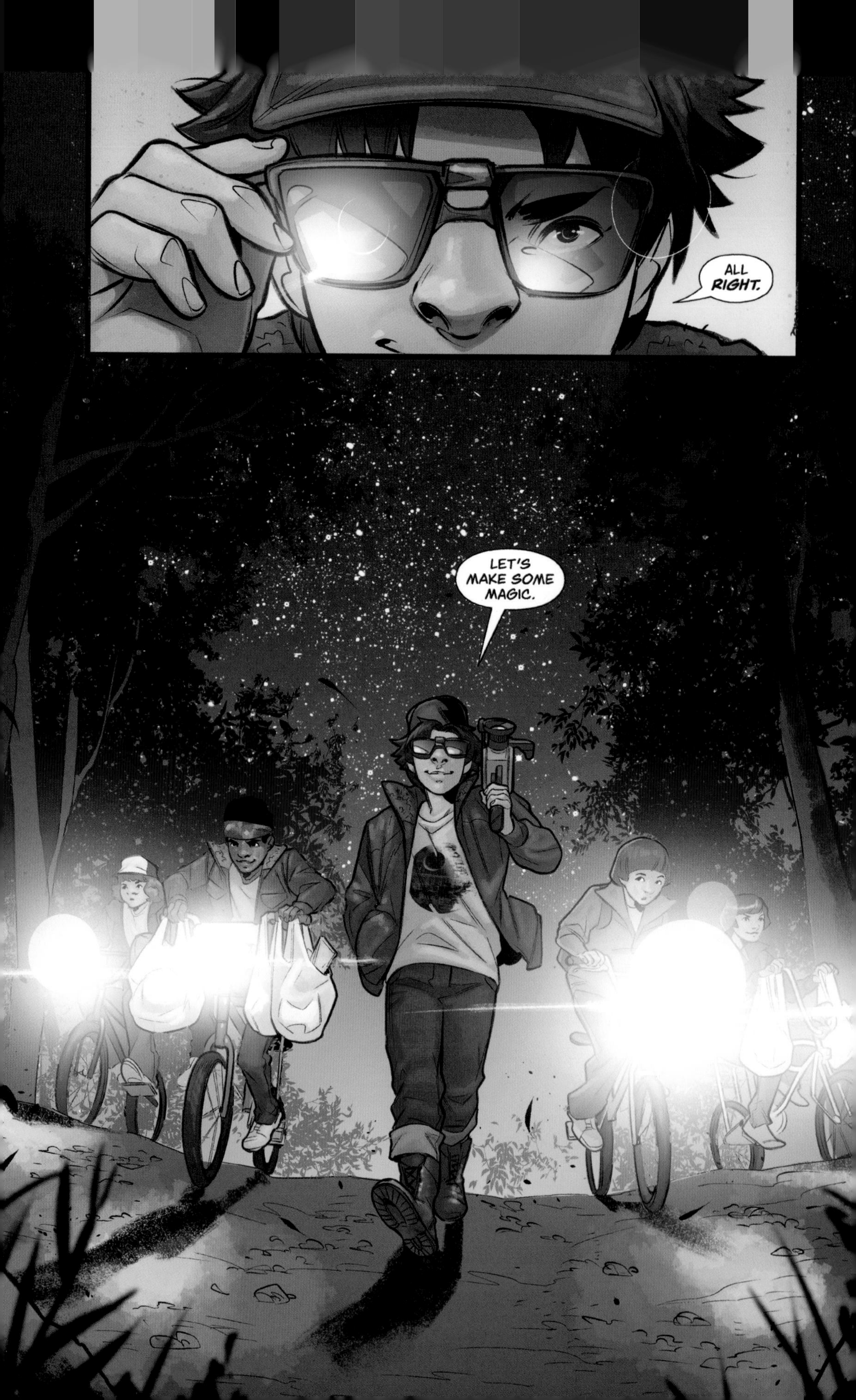
ALL RIGHT.
LET'S MAKE SOME MAGIC.

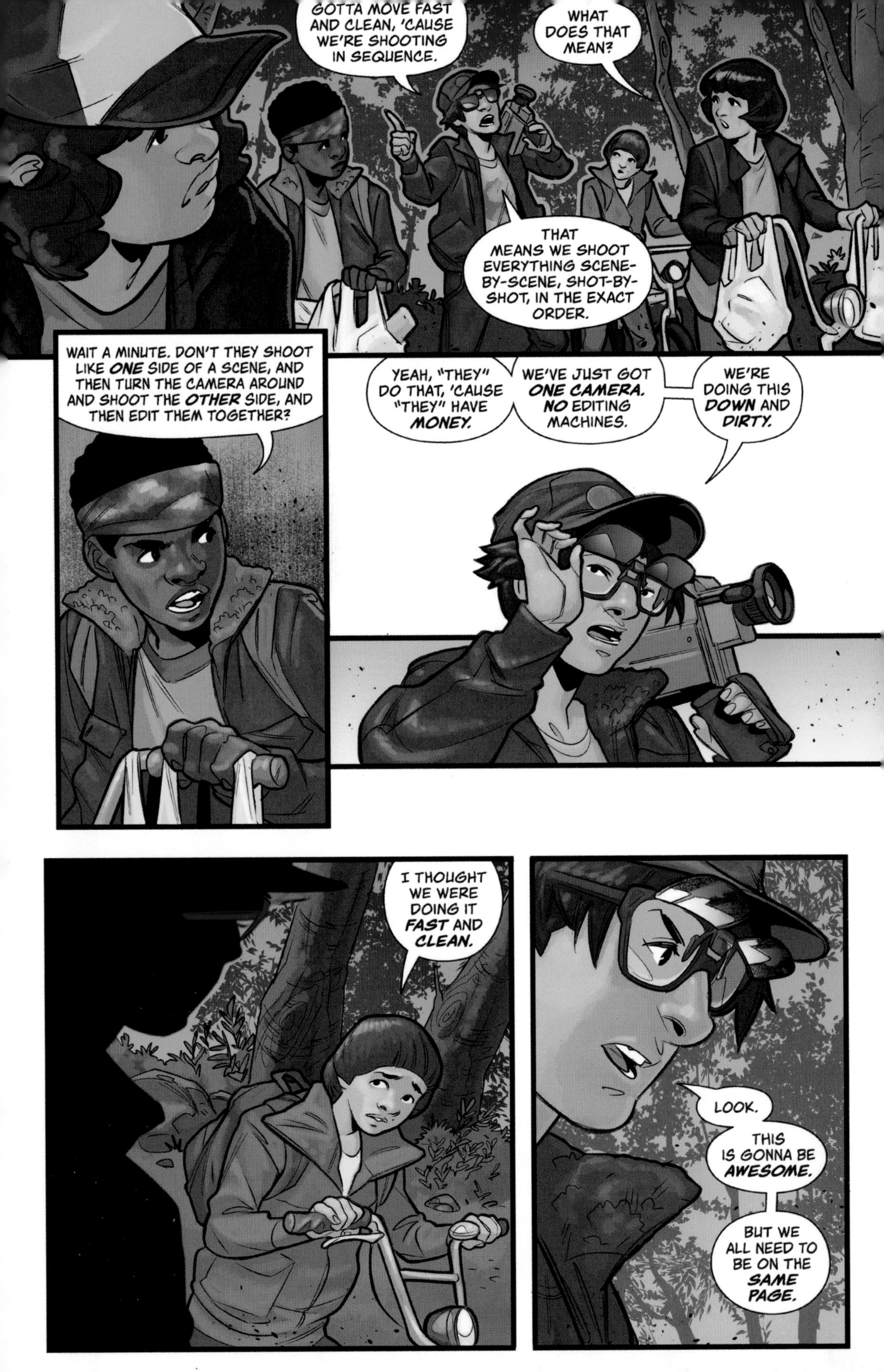
GOTTA MOVE FAST AND CLEAN, 'CAUSE WE'RE SHOOTING IN SEQUENCE.
WHAT DOES THAT MEAN?
THAT MEANS WE SHOOT EVERYTHING SCENE-BY-SCENE, SHOT-BY-SHOT, IN THE EXACT ORDER.
WAIT A MINUTE. DON'T THEY SHOOT LIKE ONE SIDE OF A SCENE, AND THEN TURN THE CAMERA AROUND AND SHOOT THE OTHER SIDE, AND THEN EDIT THEM TOGETHER?
YEAH, "THEY" DO THAT, 'CAUSE "THEY" HAVE MONEY.
WE'VE JUST GOT ONE CAMERA. NO EDITING MACHINES.
WE'RE DOING THIS DOWN AND DIRTY.
I THOUGHT WE WERE DOING IT FAST AND CLEAN.
LOOK.
THIS IS GONNA BE AWESOME.
BUT WE ALL NEED TO BE ON THE SAME PAGE.

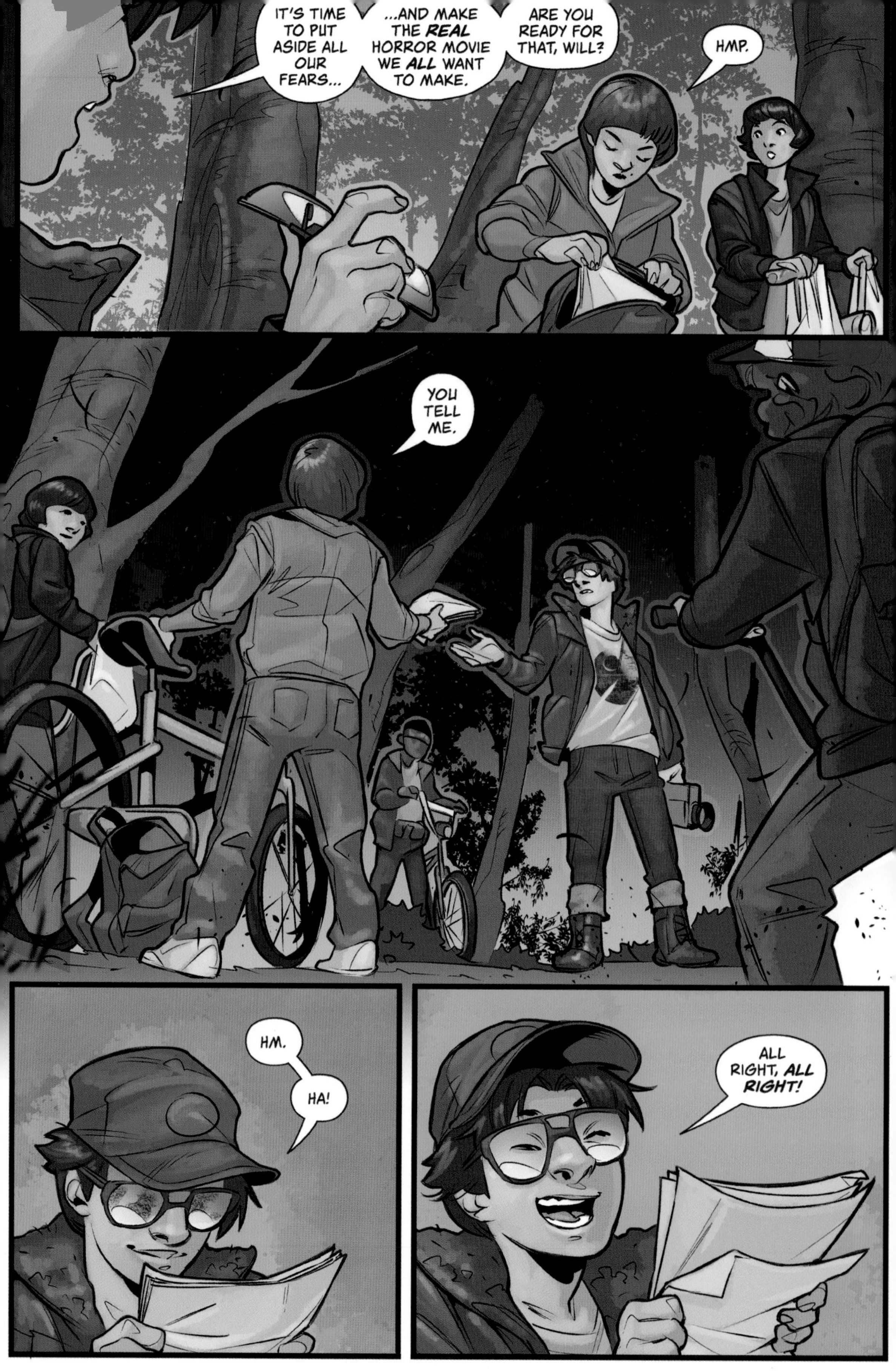
IT'S TIME TO PUT ASIDE ALL OUR FEARS...
...AND MAKE THE REAL HORROR MOVIE WE ALL WANT TO MAKE.
ARE YOU READY FOR THAT, WILL?
HMP.
YOU TELL ME.
HM.
HA!
ALL RIGHT, ALL RIGHT!

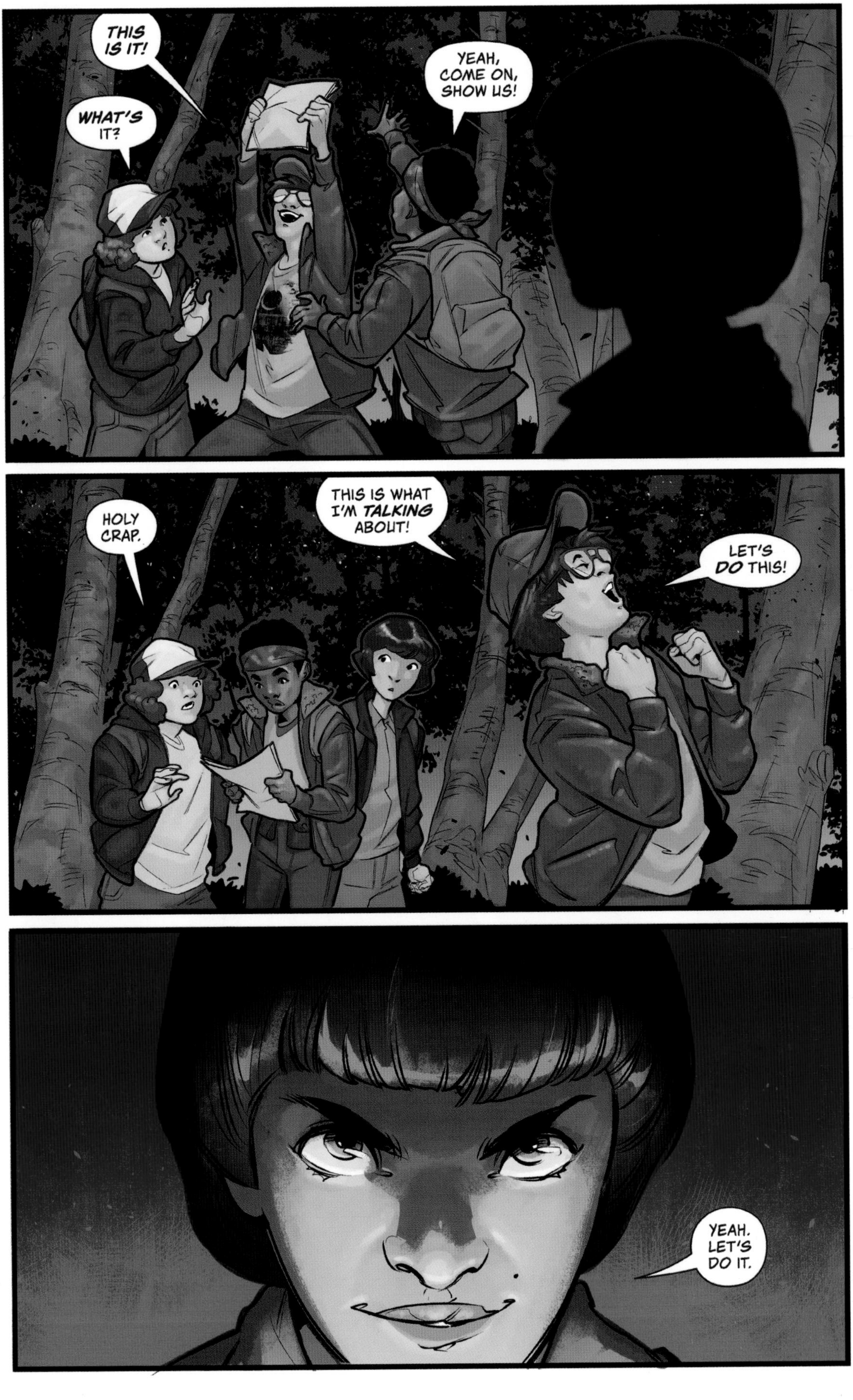
THIS IS IT!
WHAT'S IT?
YEAH, COME ON, SHOW US!
HOLY CRAP.
THIS IS WHAT I'M TALKING ABOUT!
LET'S DO THIS!
YEAH. LET'S DO IT.

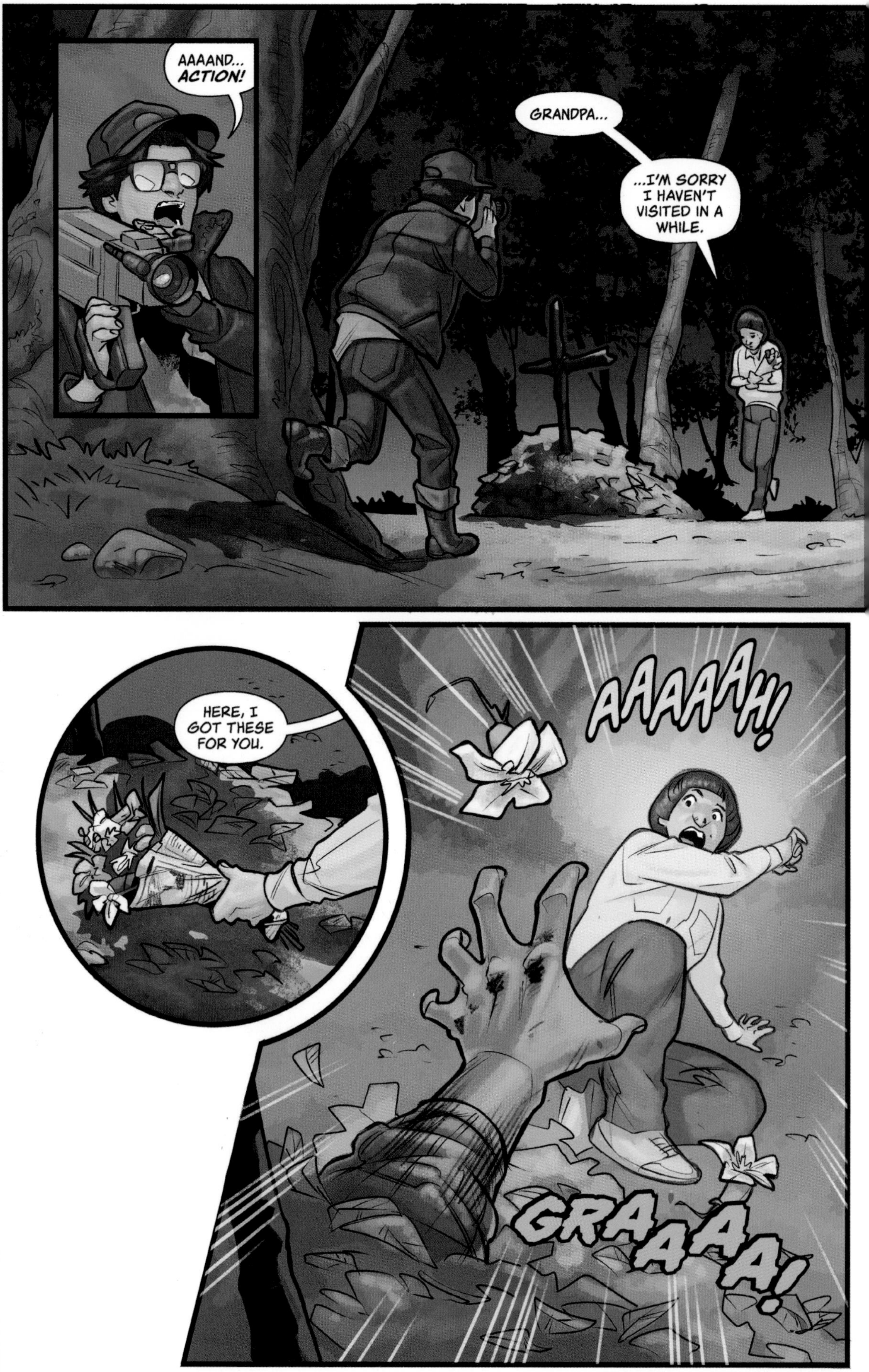
AAAAND... *ACTION!*
GRANDPA...
...I'M SORRY I HAVEN'T VISITED IN A WHILE.
HERE, I GOT THESE FOR YOU.
AAAAAH!
GRAAAAA!

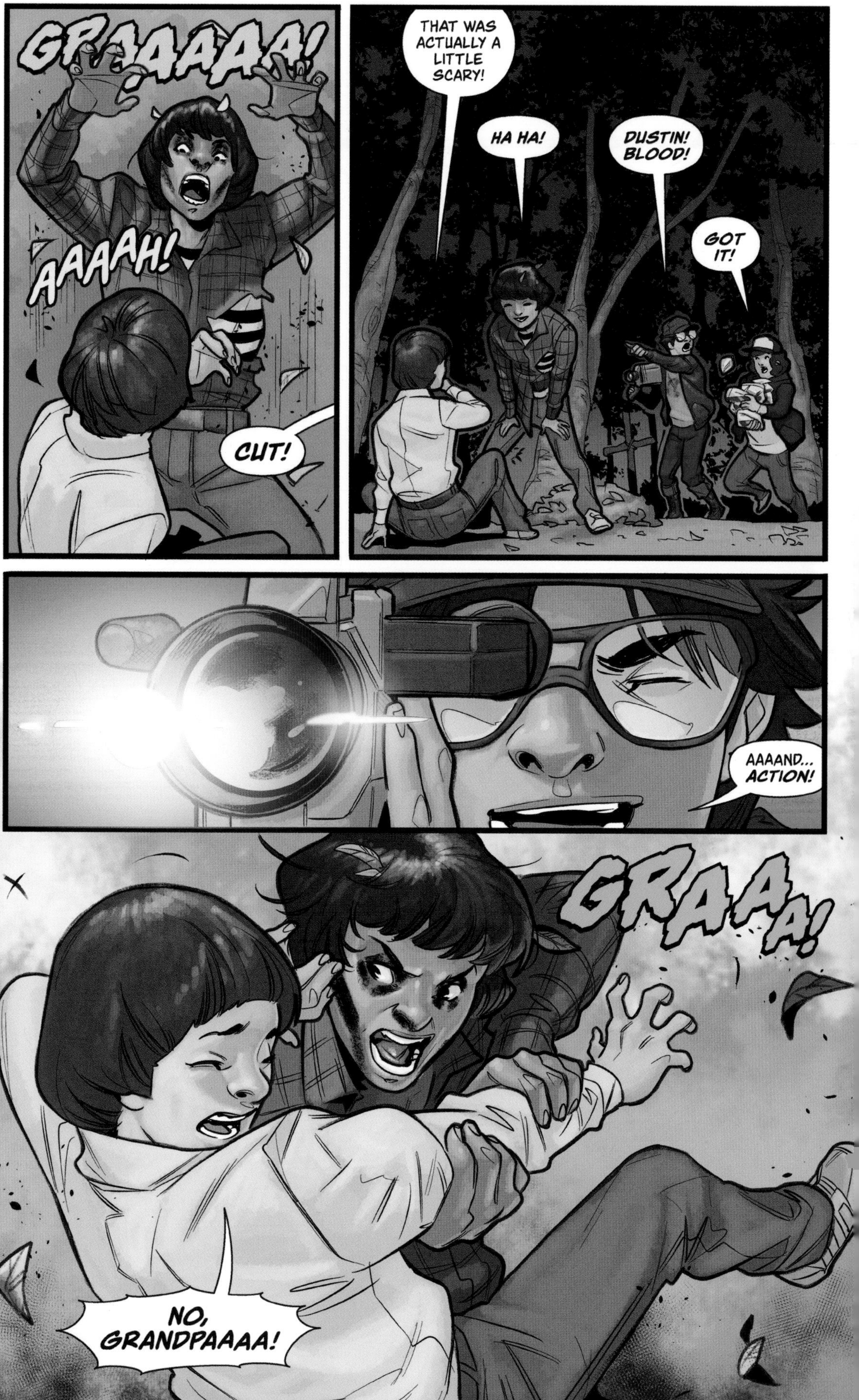
GRAAAAA!
AAAAH!
CUT!
THAT WAS ACTUALLY A LITTLE SCARY!
HA HA!
DUSTIN! BLOOD!
GOT IT!
AAAAND... ACTION!
GRAAA!
NO, GRANDPAAAA!

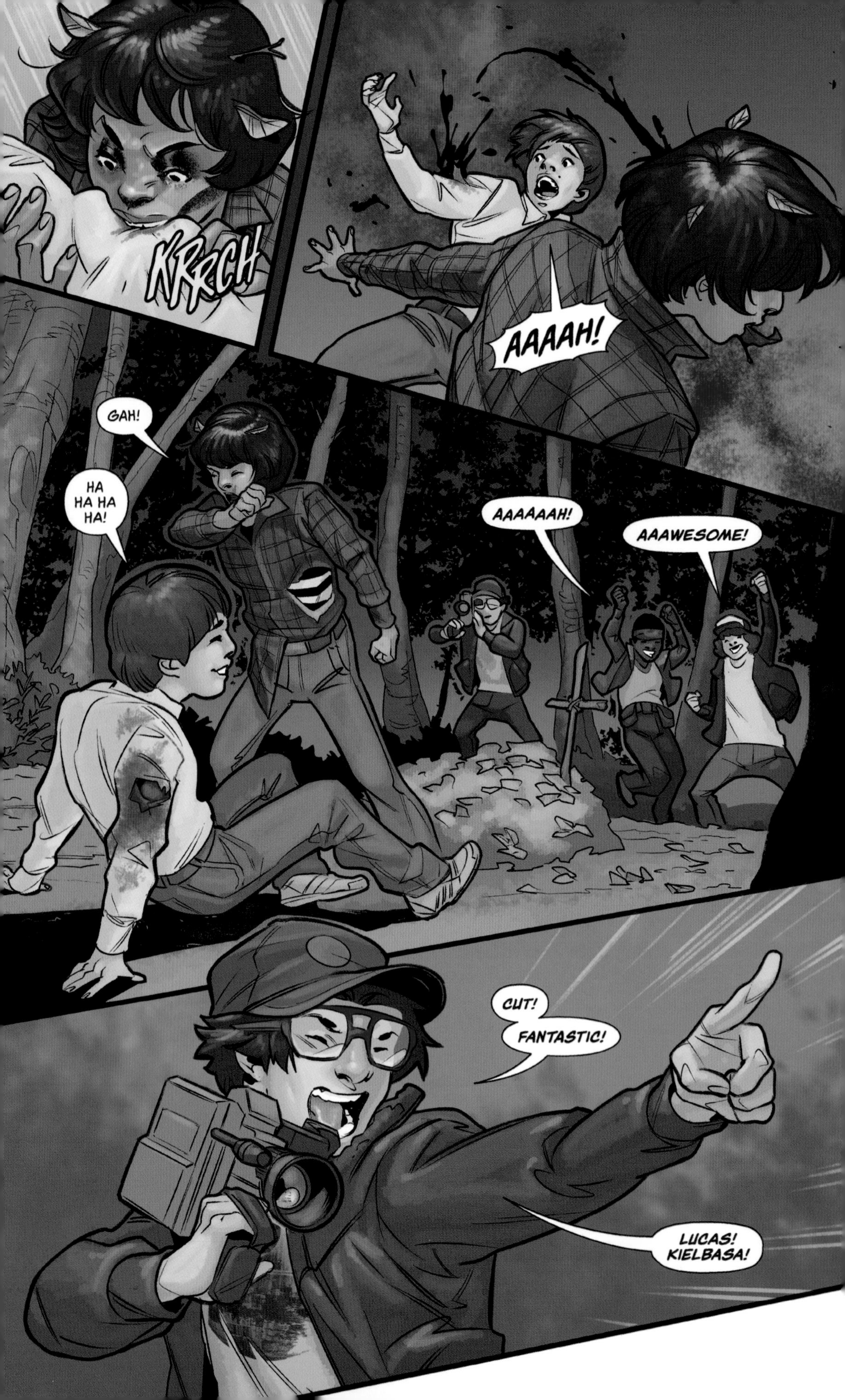
KRRCH
AAAAH!
GAH!
HA HA HA HA!
AAAAAAH!
AAAWESOME!
CUT!
FANTASTIC!
LUCAS! KIELBASA!

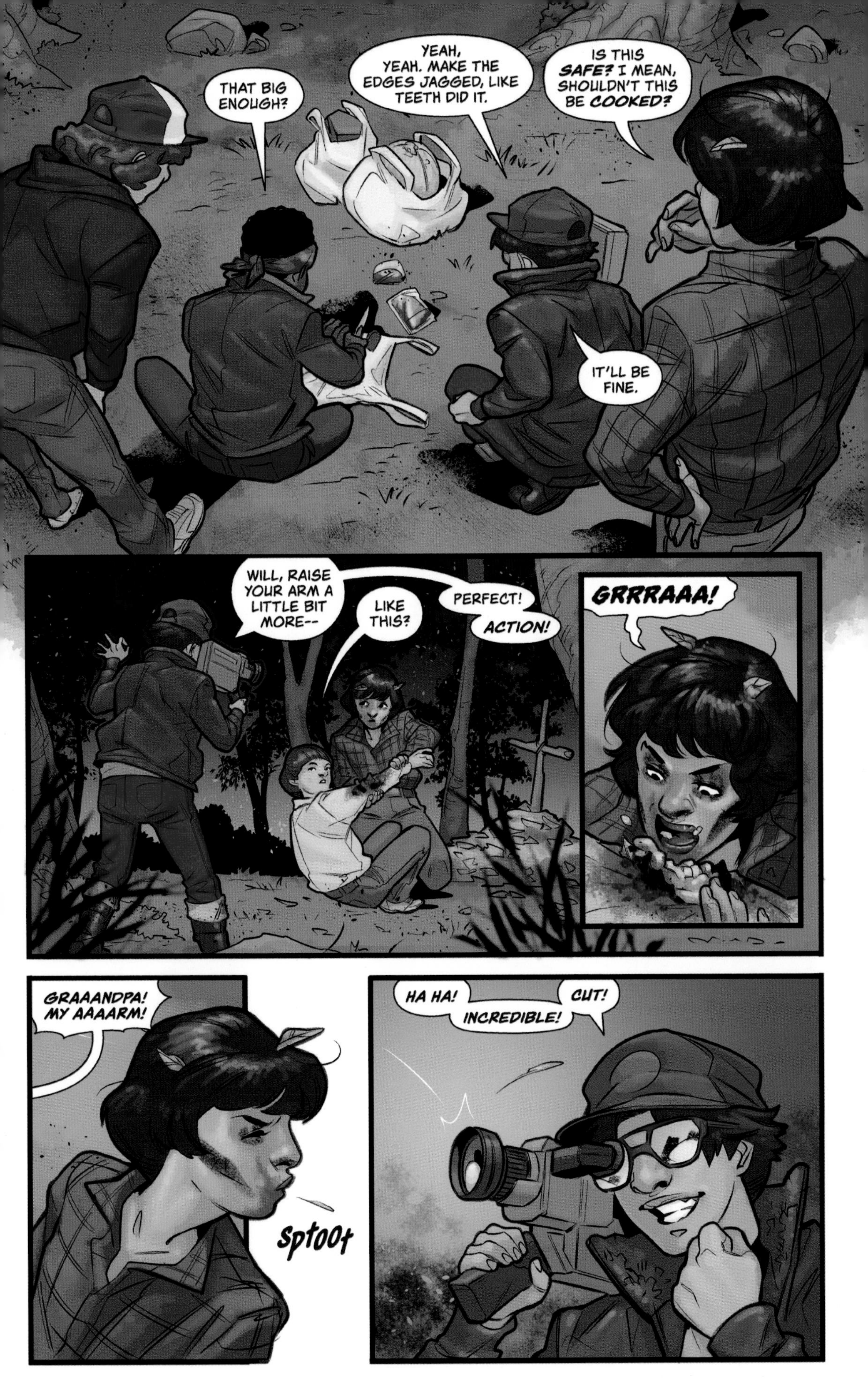
THAT BIG ENOUGH?
YEAH, YEAH. MAKE THE EDGES JAGGED, LIKE TEETH DID IT.
IS THIS SAFE? I MEAN, SHOULDN'T THIS BE COOKED?
IT'LL BE FINE.
WILL, RAISE YOUR ARM A LITTLE BIT MORE--
LIKE THIS?
PERFECT!
ACTION!
GRRRAAA!
GRAAANDPA! MY AAAARM!
sptoot
HA HA!
INCREDIBLE!
CUT!

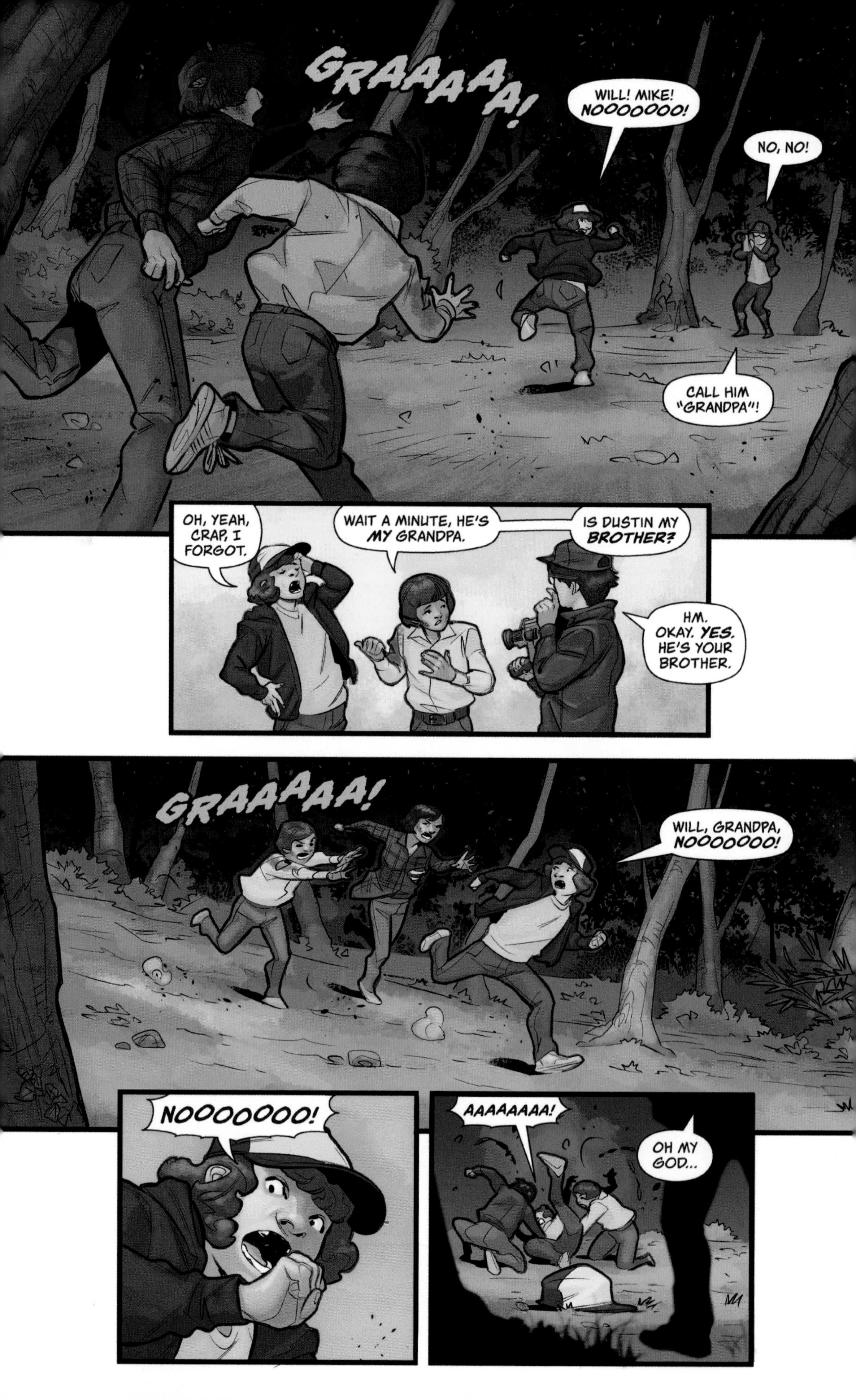
GRAAAAAA!
WILL! MIKE! NOOOOOOO!
NO, NO!
CALL HIM "GRANDPA"!
OH, YEAH, CRAP, I FORGOT.
WAIT A MINUTE, HE'S MY GRANDPA.
IS DUSTIN MY BROTHER?
HM. OKAY. YES. HE'S YOUR BROTHER.
GRAAAAAA!
WILL, GRANDPA, NOOOOOOO!
NOOOOOOO!
AAAAAAAA!
OH MY GOD...

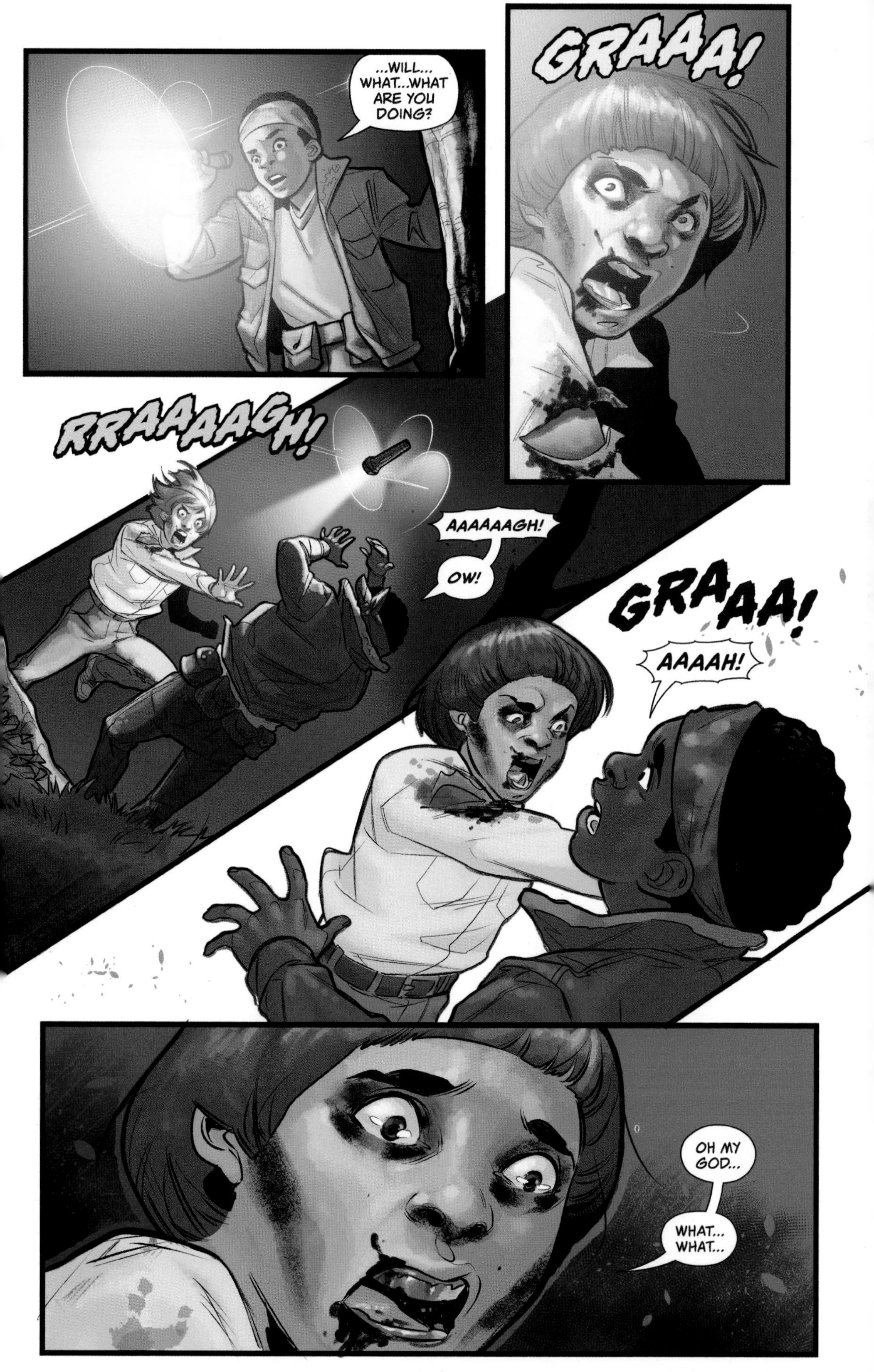
...WILL...
WHAT...WHAT
ARE YOU
DOING?
GRAAAA!
RRAAAAAAGH!
AAAAAAGH!
OW!
GRAAAA!
AAAAH!
OH MY
GOD...
WHAT...
WHAT...

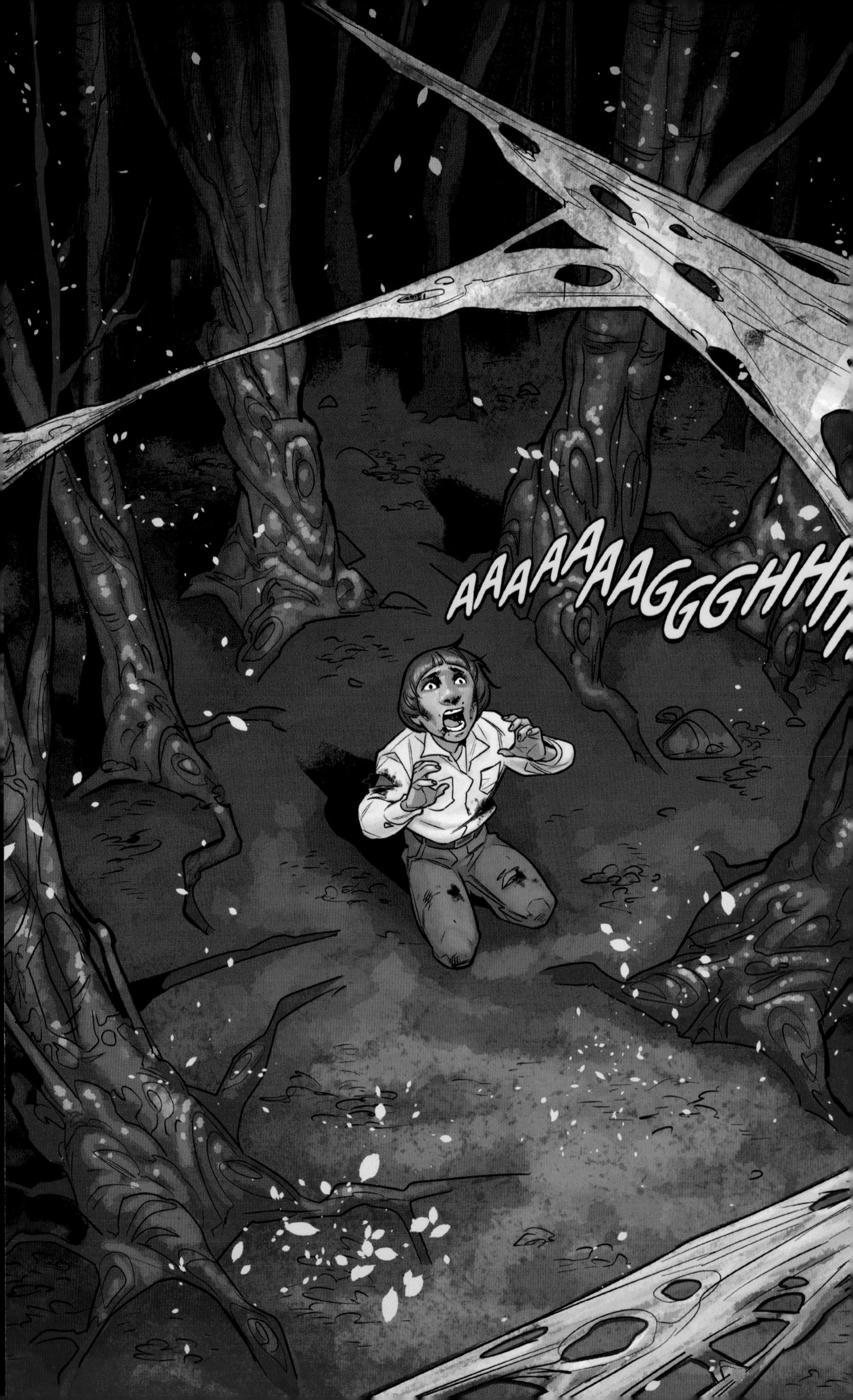
AAAAAAAGGGHHH

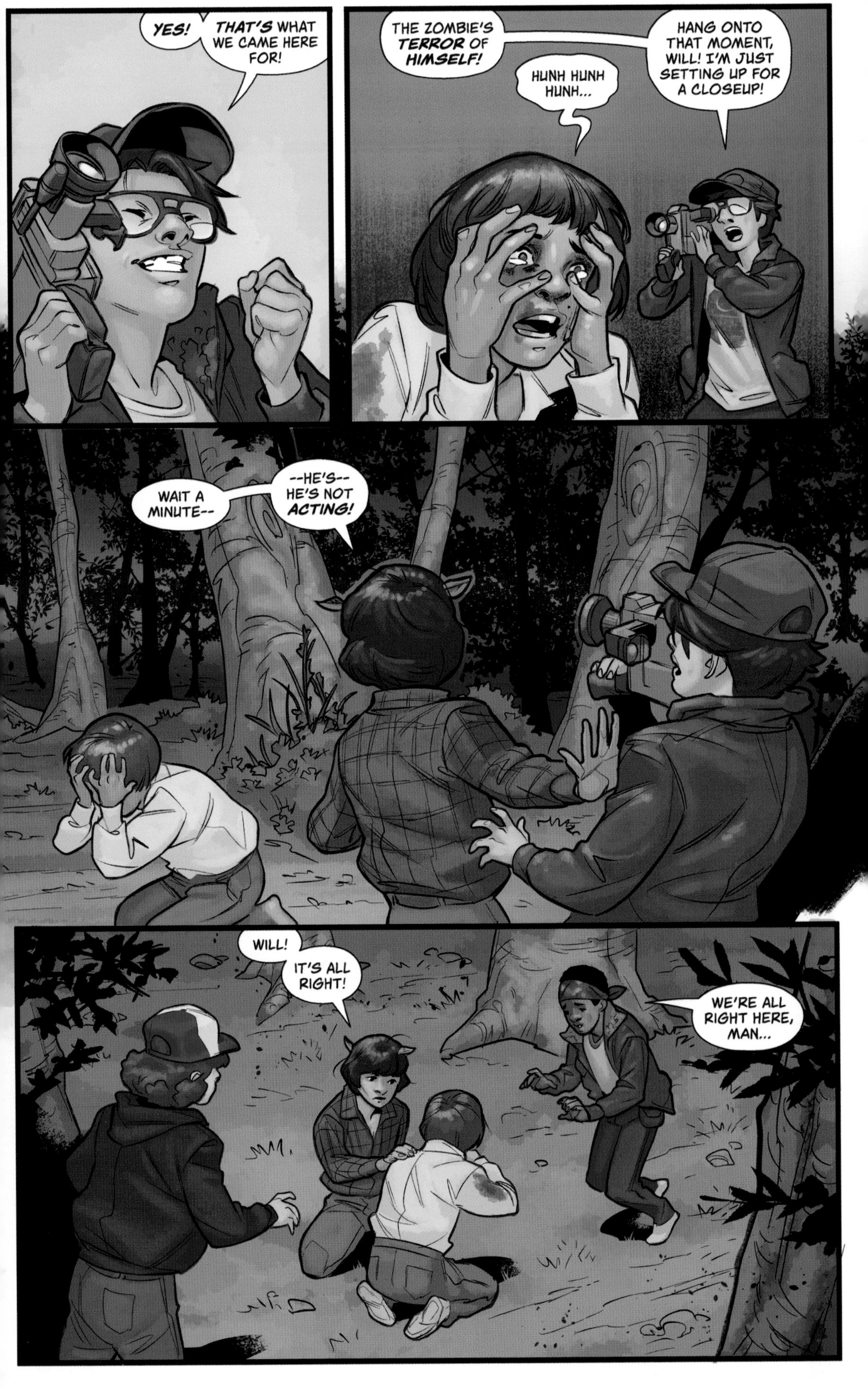
YES!
THAT'S WHAT WE CAME HERE FOR!
THE ZOMBIE'S TERROR OF HIMSELF!
HANG ONTO THAT MOMENT, WILL! I'M JUST SETTING UP FOR A CLOSEUP!
HUNH HUNH HUNH...
WAIT A MINUTE--
--HE'S-- HE'S NOT ACTING!
WILL!
IT'S ALL RIGHT!
WE'RE ALL RIGHT HERE, MAN...

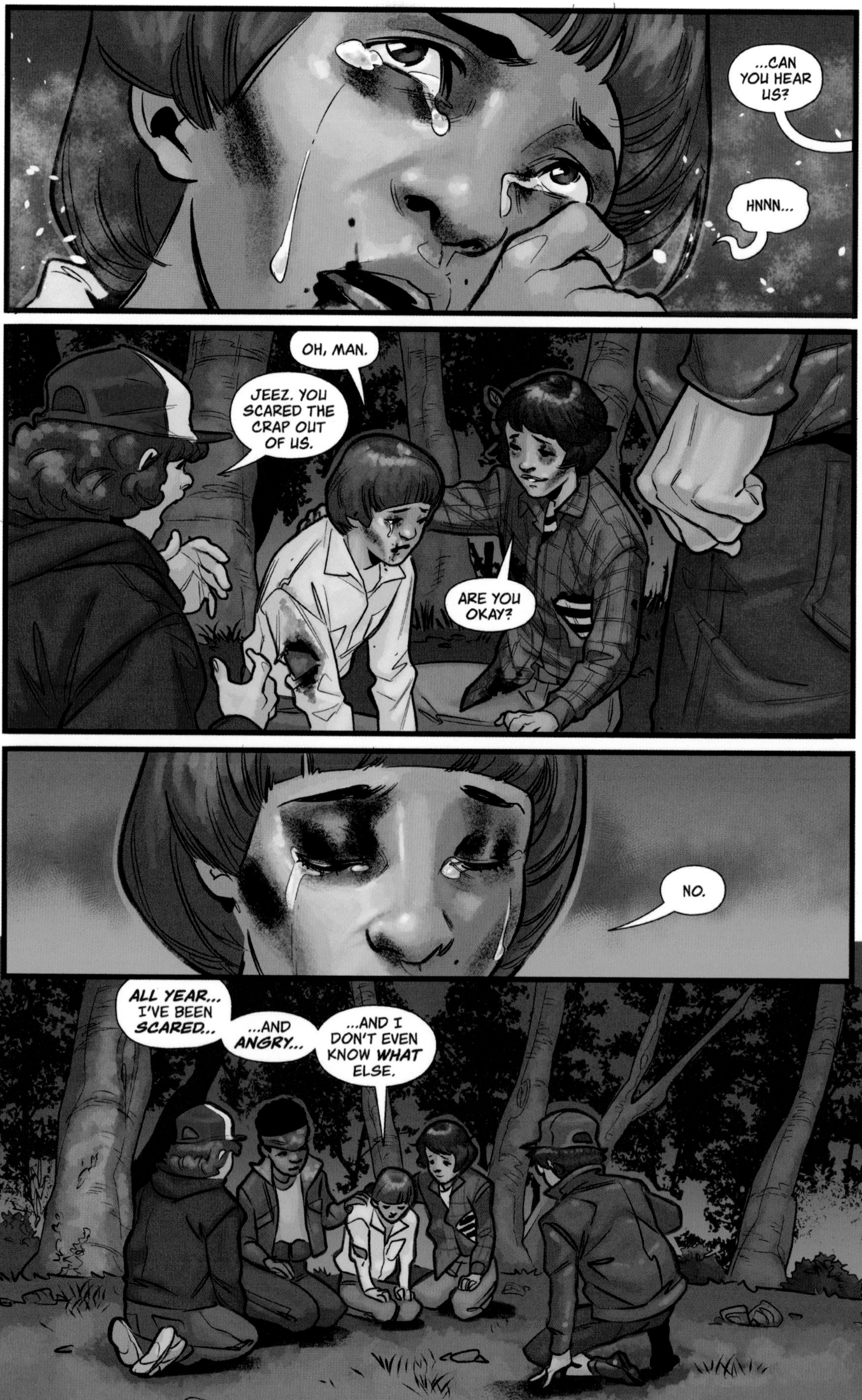
...CAN YOU HEAR US?
HNNN...
OH, MAN.
JEEZ. YOU SCARED THE CRAP OUT OF US.
ARE YOU OKAY?
NO.
ALL YEAR... I'VE BEEN SCARED...
...AND ANGRY...
...AND I DON'T EVEN KNOW WHAT ELSE.

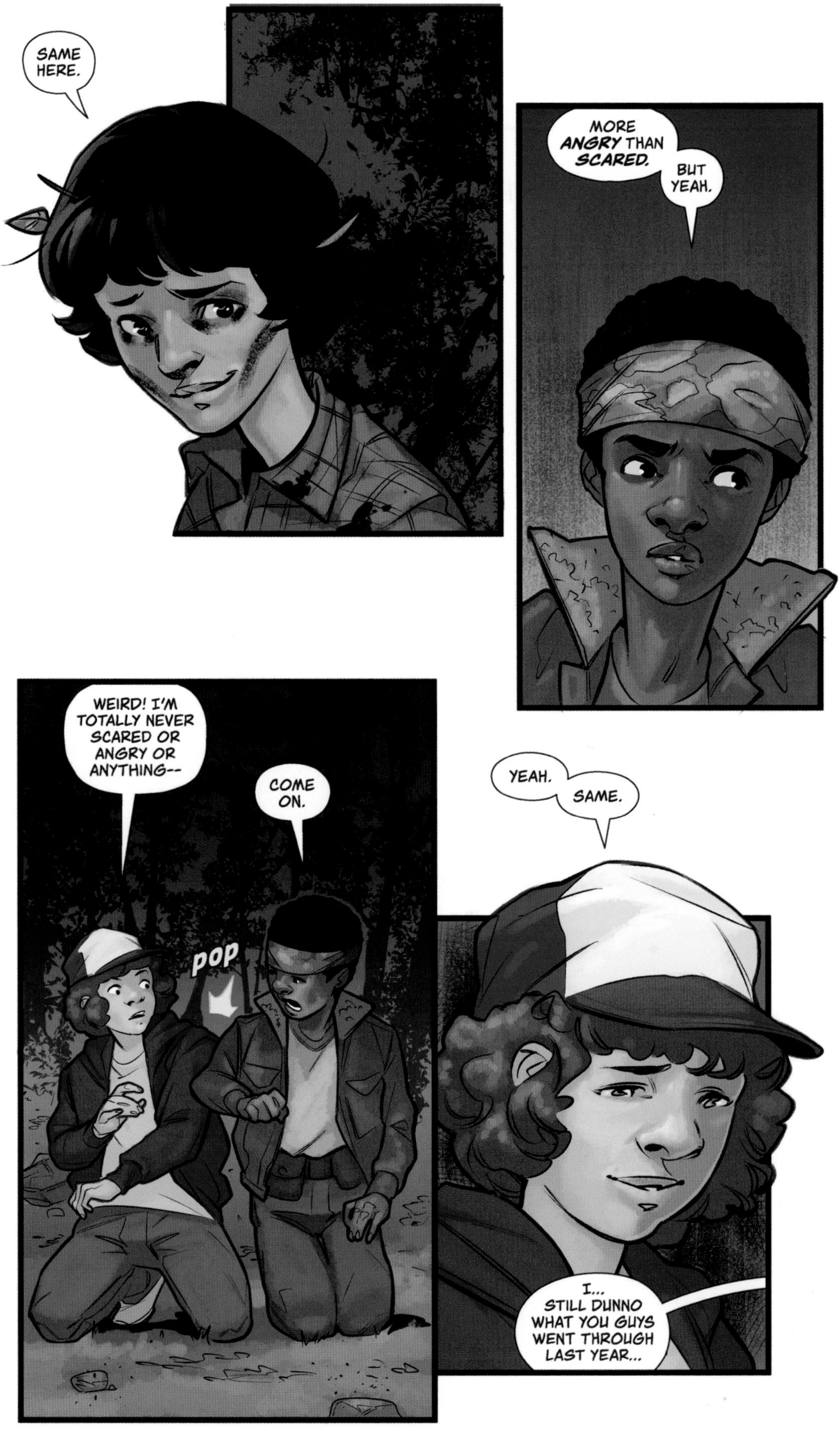
SAME HERE.
MORE ANGRY THAN SCARED.
BUT YEAH.
WEIRD! I'M TOTALLY NEVER SCARED OR ANGRY OR ANYTHING--
COME ON.
pop
YEAH.
SAME.
I... STILL DUNNO WHAT YOU GUYS WENT THROUGH LAST YEAR...

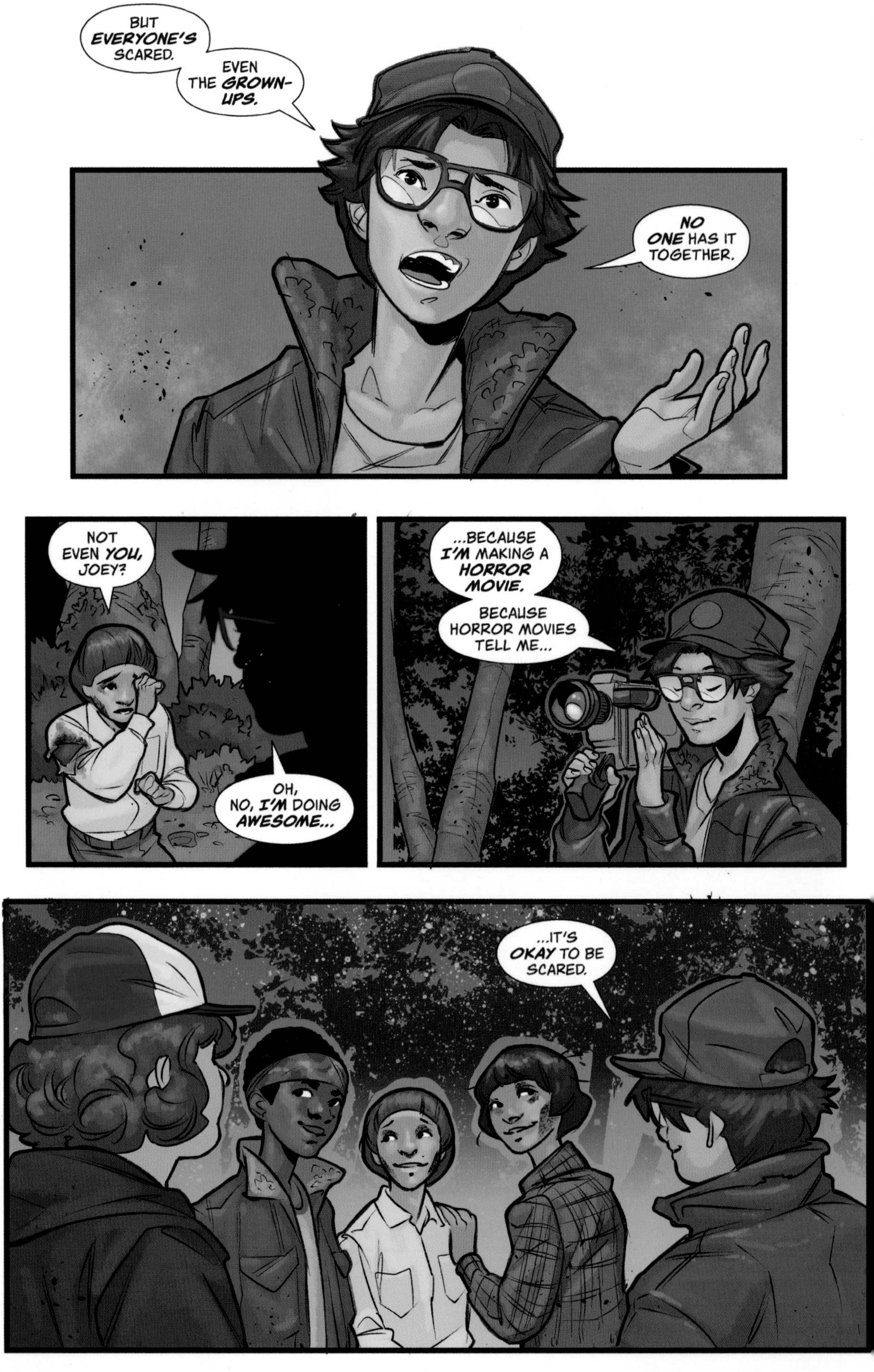
BUT EVERYONE'S SCARED.
EVEN THE GROWN-UPS.
NO ONE HAS IT TOGETHER.
NOT EVEN YOU, JOEY?
OH, NO, I'M DOING AWESOME...
...BECAUSE I'M MAKING A HORROR MOVIE.
BECAUSE HORROR MOVIES TELL ME...
...IT'S OKAY TO BE SCARED.

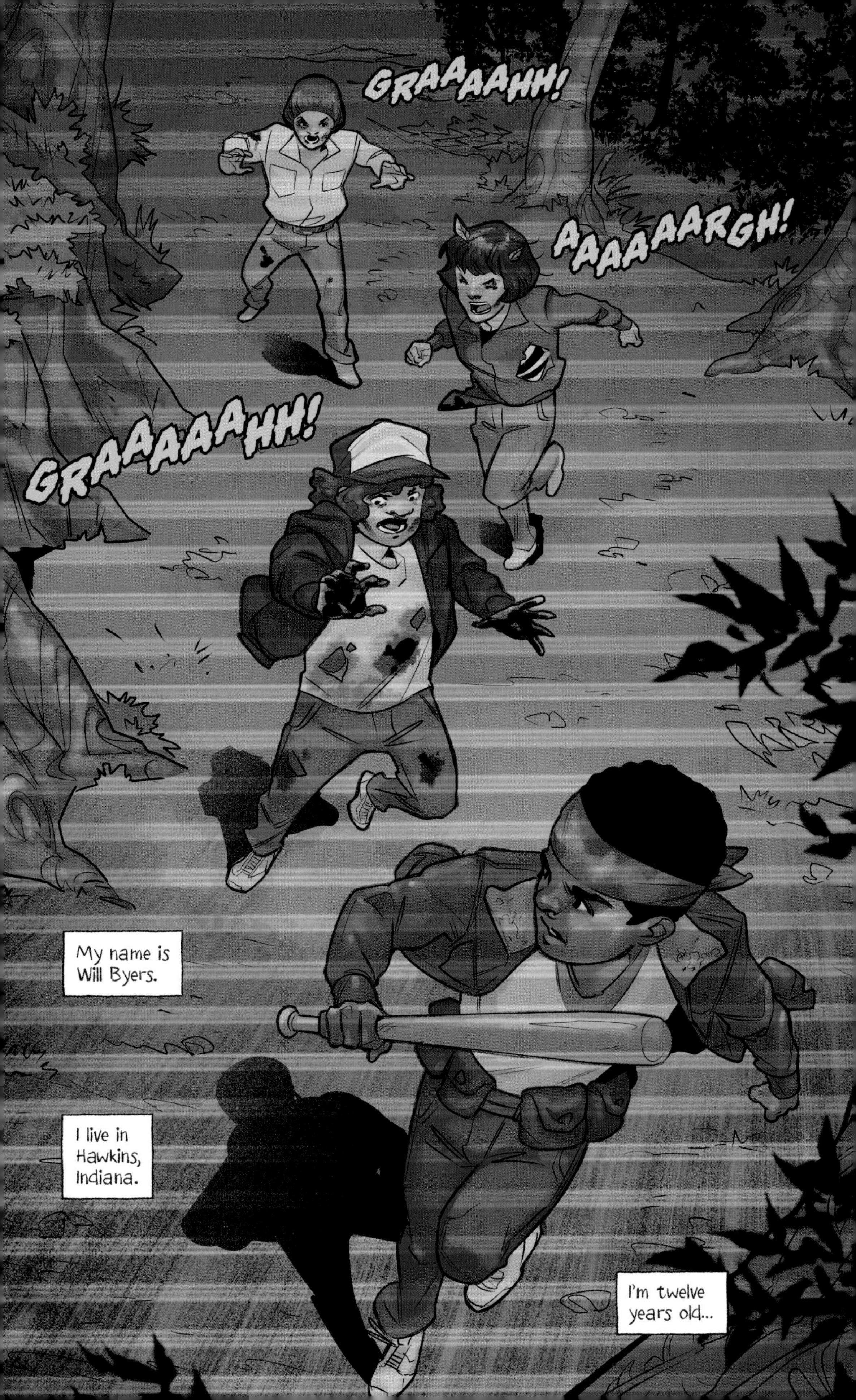
GRAAAAHH!
AAAAAARGH!
GRAAAAAHH!
My name is Will Byers.
I live in Hawkins, Indiana.
I'm twelve years old...

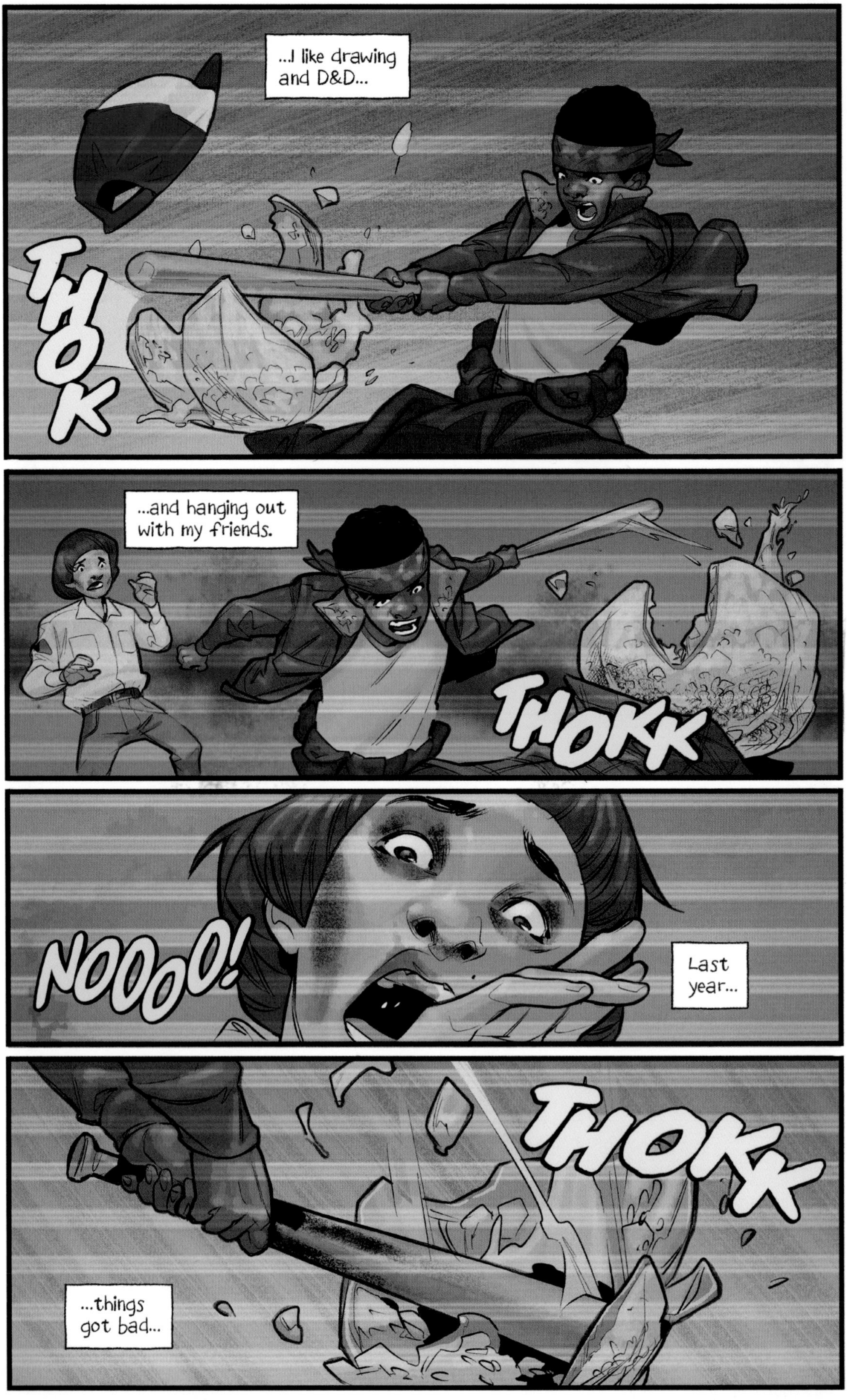
...I like drawing and D&D...
THOK
...and hanging out with my friends.
THOKK
NOOOOO!
Last year...
THOKK
...things got bad...

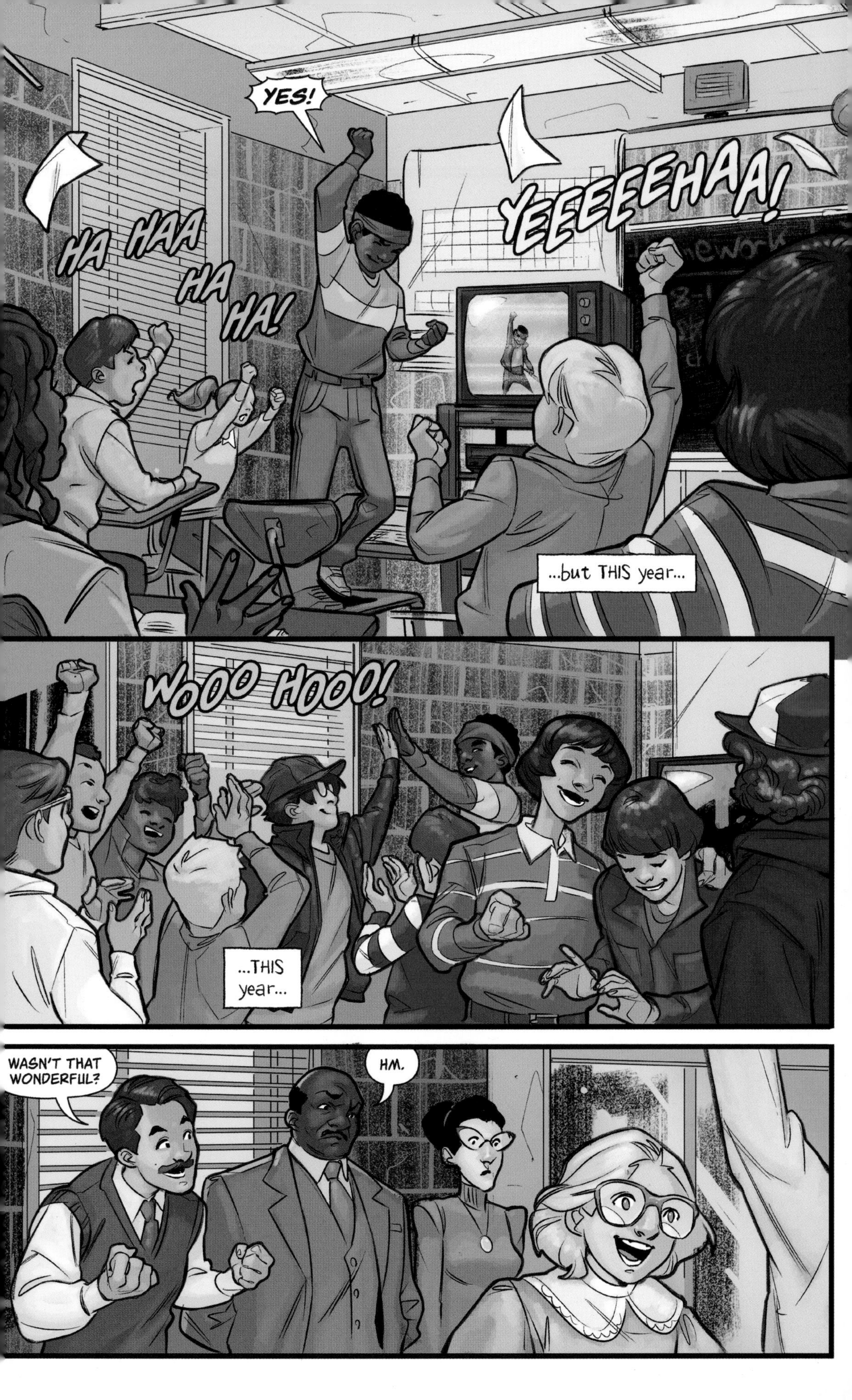
YES!
HA HAA HA HA!
YEEEEEHAA!
...but THIS year...
WOOO HOOO!
...THIS year...
WASN'T THAT WONDERFUL?
HM.

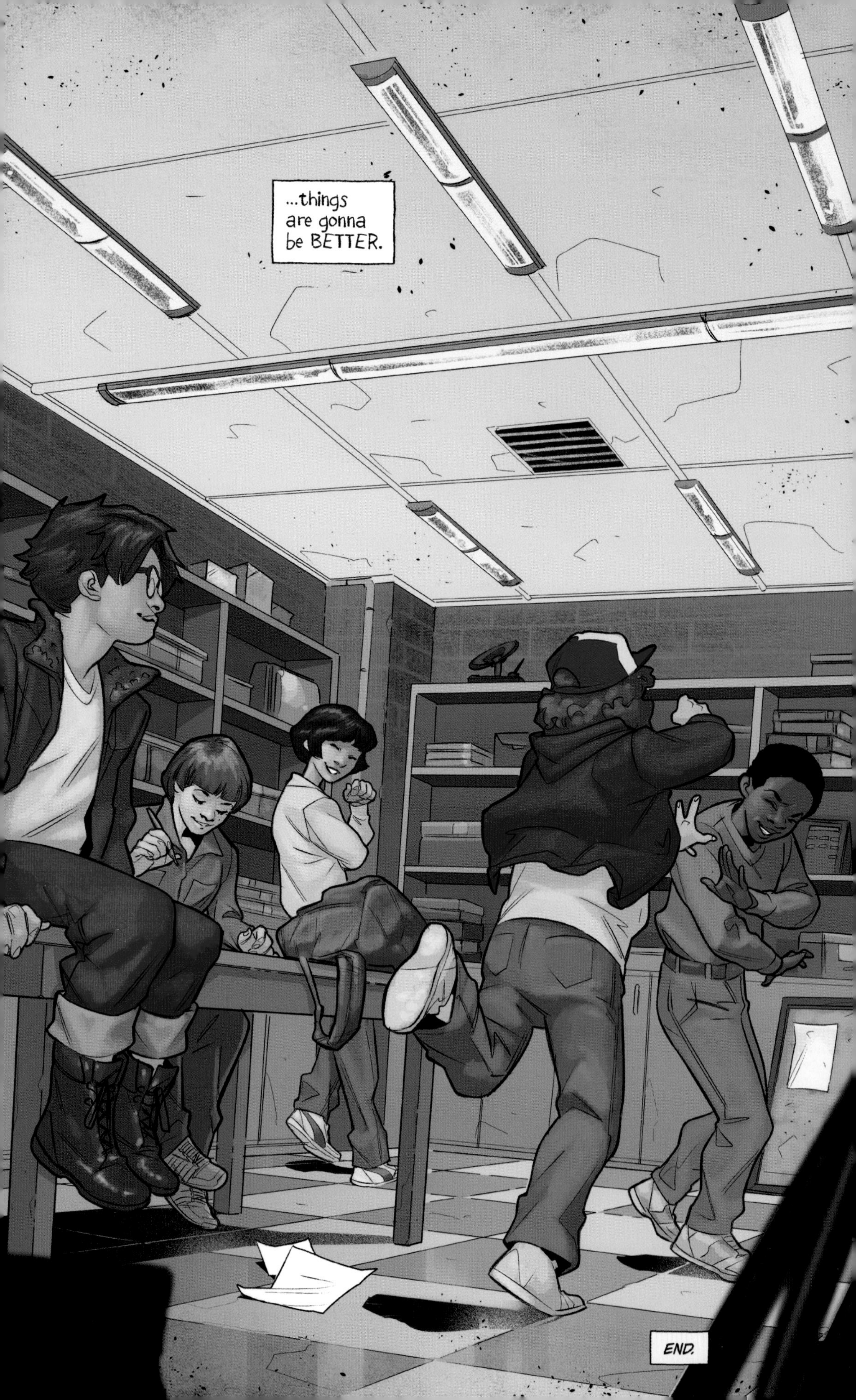
...things are gonna be BETTER.
END.